John's Remarkable Journey

Copyright © 2008 mike young
All rights reserved.
ISBN: 1-4196-8678-X
ISBN-13: 978-1419686788

MIKE YOUNG

JOHN'S REMARKABLE JOURNEY

2008

John's Remarkable Journey

TABLE OF CONTENTS

Page

LIST OF ILLUSTRATIONS

Illustrations by Marcia E. Young

To My Dear Friend, Henri.

CHAPTER 1
A Gift

It was a blustery, late autumn afternoon as Dick stared out his office window, mesmerized by little sailboats racing across the choppy waters of the Charles. He dreaded the coming of winter and hoped the new patient would somehow bring him a reprieve from that unpleasant season.

"I used to sail," John said, with an air of obvious sadness.

"Did you enjoy it?" Dick asked, not sure of where to go yet.

With a look that clearly revealed his underlying discontent, John finally replied after a long delay. "Immensely," he said.

"Immensely?" Dick wondered how this could be the case as he seemed so gloomy when he said it.

"It's the feeling of being free. The only sounds you hear come from waves slapping against the bow or lufting sails."

John Holmes was a man in his late-fifties, reasonably physically fit and well mannered, a successful professional, yet Dick easily detected the struggle inside. They talked more about his adventures sailing the coastal waters of New England and he seemed a little happier until they got to the part about his wife. She hardly ever went sailing with him, perhaps because she didn't like to sail or maybe she just didn't want to spend time with him. John wasn't sure though and this was one of the things that had caused him some sadness for a long time.

It was at that point in their conversation that John first revealed to Dick why he wanted his help. It seemed, in addition to his recent divorce and being fired from his job, he had another reason.

"I really came here because I want to discover the true meaning of life," John said.

This was such a fundamental human longing and Dick couldn't help but chuckle a little at the enormity of the task. None of his patients had ever asked his help in solving such a big riddle.

"I mean my life, not everybody's life," John explained.

Dick agreed that was more manageable and suggested they begin by making a list of the usual things that were important to men, like friends, family and the activities he enjoyed. They should talk about John's marriage and career, as these, too, were significant events that would have contributed to the ultimate meaning of his life.

"What about the big one?" Dick asked.

"You mean taxes?"

"No," Dick said smiling a little. "The other big one."

"Death?"

"We're going to have to talk about it."

"Okay," John acknowledged with a big sigh.

It was clear to Dick that this wasn't another routine counseling situation, as John sincerely did want to understand the meaning of his life. This was fascinating to Dick and he began to look forward to their meetings as much as he thought John did.

***

They began with hunting, one of John's once favorite sports.

"You enjoyed it because of the rituals?" Dick wondered.

"Yes. Checking our gear, cleaning the guns, studying the maps, speculating on our luck," he said. "Rituals prepare you."

Dick hadn't ever thought about hunting from that perspective, but it made sense to him, in an ancient archetypal sort of way. One thing led to another and soon they found themselves engaged in a serious discussion about life and death.

"The taking of a life seemed a sacred act. It made me wonder about my own mortality," John admitted. "And thinking about death makes you wonder where your spirit goes."

"Where do you think it goes?"

"I'm not sure," John shrugged.

John didn't seem ready to talk more about his immortality and it was simpler to talk about fishing. Dick noted that it wasn't as easy to feel sorry for a slimy fish as it was for a gentle deer bounding peacefully through the woods. And unlike hunting, fishing was something John still liked to do on occasion and their discussion brought back a childhood incident John felt was particularly poignant in his life. Having grown up in New York City, Dick never went fishing so he listened to him with some personal interest, feeling all along that John's stories were on the typical path the human psyche takes into life's big questions.

"When I was a kid, I used to fish with my best friend and his dad, this gruff old Marine. I liked the man, but I was never really sure if I should be afraid of him."

"Afraid?" Dick said, considering that the man may have been mean to the kids.

"We used the old fashioned reels which were tricky to cast without getting the line all snarled up."

"And your friend's dad was in charge of untangling them."

"Constantly."

"What are you smiling at?"

"I was just remembering one time when we were fishing at the creek and Bobby got his reel all screwed up, for the umpteenth time. His dad got angry as usual and went to kick him in the butt but missed and slipped down the muddy bank into the water."

"What happened then?" Dick asked smiling as he imagined the comic frustration of the situation.

"He climbed out, yelling at us, so we ran away from him. Then he chased us, pretending to be angry. We had great fun evading him, keeping up the game."

Dick could see the fond memories flickering in John's eyes. "You guys still go fishing together?"

"No."

"Why not?"

"Bobby was killed in the same war I fought in," John replied, showing some old emotions that had welled up inside.

"Oh," was all Dick could muster at the moment, preferring to come back to this difficult subject when John was ready.

Finally, John broke their silence as he got up to look out at the sailboats. "Even so, I've always liked the way those old times made me feel."

"Why is that?"

"Things were simple then. Life was filled with sweet spots."

This immediately reminded Dick of how much he used to love to play stickball in the street near his house. John's mention of the sweet spot recalled that exhilaration of connecting perfectly. "What's better than hitting a home run?" Dick asked.

"Not much," John smiled, suddenly shaking his head. "I still can't believe they just announced, out of a clear blue sky, I was being forced into early retirement. Imagine that," he said, throwing his hands up into the air and changing his expression into a sarcastic grimace. "Where did all the sweet spots go?"

They had been immersed in such pleasant reverie remembering their childhoods it seemed a shame to ruin the feeling with a serious discussion about job problems or the loss of friends. They would have time for all that as they worked through the plusses and minuses that gave meaning to John's life. So Dick ended the session and John was happy to leave remembering a few of the good times in his life.

***

John stared anxiously from across the room as Dick quickly jotted down a last few notes about his previous patient. He was going to apologize for making him wait, but John spoke before Dick had the chance.

"I'm going to die," John blurted out.

He said it with such melodramatic conviction that Dick couldn't help but burst out with a laugh, but the look on John's face suggested he really wasn't kidding.

"I'm sorry," Dick said, regretting his mistake.

"I mean it," John said emphatically. "The doctor said I have cancer and it will kill me."

"Oh God, John. I'm sorry," Dick said, plainly seeing the pain he was in. "We have cures for cancer," he quickly added with hope in his voice.

"They say it's advanced."

"Metastasized?"

"Yeah."

Dick leaned back in his chair and let out a big sigh. Considering that the man's wife had divorced him, his boss had fired him and now his doctor told him he was going to die from cancer, things weren't going very well for John.

"I think you should get a second opinion."

"I'm going to see a surgeon tomorrow."

"What about an oncologist?"

"Friday," John replied.

"Let's wait to hear what they have to say."

"Wait for what?" he asked Dick.

John was still in shock. Dick made the mistake of thinking too far ahead about how to help him through this even bigger problem. He should have been thinking about what to say to get him to calm down.

"I mean there's a lot for us to talk about, after you find out, for sure," Dick answered.

"There already was a lot to talk about, before this happened," John said, almost yelling at Dick.

"You must be feeling more of a sense of urgency now," Dick suggested. "We can prioritize things."

"You mean, so that I can figure out the meaning of my life before I really do die?"

"I didn't mean it exactly like that."

"I don't even feel like I'm going to die," John shrugged, but seeming to agree with Dick. "But, you're right," John added. "Let's keep going."

The man had a lot of fight left in him but, clearly at this late point in his life, he was more alone than he wanted to be.

"Who else have you told?" Dick asked.

"No one."

"What about your wife?"

"You mean ex-wife," he winced.

Dick's expression suggested John could do better than that.

"I hate to admit it, but I did call her."

"What did she say?"

"Her voice mail said she was on an extended vacation and to leave a message."

"Did you?"

"No."

"Why not?"

"I don't think she would care."

"I think she would."

"You don't know her."

They talked for quite awhile about his marriage, the good times as well as the bad, and Dick finally convinced him to give her another call, but doubted he ever would. John only agreed so Dick would stop bugging him.

"I'd still like to figure out the true meaning of my life, Dick."

"What do you think we should do?" Dick asked, hoping that John had an idea because he didn't, not at that moment anyway, but he should have after all those years of psychiatric practice. John didn't say anything, so Dick ended up going first.

"Do you believe in life after death?" As soon as those words came out of his mouth, Dick realized maybe they shouldn't have.

"You mean, what do I believe in?"

Maybe the question hadn't been foolish after all. He really did need to know what John thought about the subject.

"Well, I'm going to die, I mean sooner than you are. Probably," he kidded.

"We could discuss what's ultimately of value?"

"Yeah," John nodded. "How do we do that?"

"What if we explore some principle philosophies?" John just shrugged. "It's a gift you know," Dick added.

"A gift? What, dying at my age?"

"When we're born, we're not given any guarantees how long we'll live. What about those guys you knew in the army? How old were they when they were killed? Nineteen, twenty?" Dick left his question hanging in the air. It was a matter of personal opinion, so there was nothing more to say. John would have to decide if he agreed or not.

"You're right, Dick, it is a gift," John admitted finally. "I have an opportunity that most people never get. I know when it's going to happen."

"We fear death," Dick replied, "because we think we'll lose our consciousness, the only perception we've ever known."

"But we don't know that for sure, do we?" John asked.

"How could we?" Dick responded. "Maybe we don't."

"What about all the jerks?" John grinned. "What happens to them?"

"They get their just rewards," Dick smiled back.

"So they don't go to heaven?"

"Correct." Dick tried to keep a straight face but John knew he was smiling underneath. But how could Dick be so sure that all the jerks wouldn't go to heaven? Preferring not to say another word for the moment, both of them silently enjoyed the idea that all the jerks in the world would definitely not go to heaven.

"The Egyptians believed in a physical afterlife," Dick continued. "And the Hindus have a fascinating certainty about all of this. They call it the coordinating principle. It's the essential activity required to expand human perception of the truth and achieve cosmic consciousness."

"What is it?"

"Breathing."

"Oh, great. So, all I have to do is not stop breathing."

"Something like that," Dick smiled a little. "And when you become one with the cosmos, your individual soul will be just a particle of the great cosmic principle."

"Just a particle?" John complained.

"Ultimately, I think we're all headed to the same place, though." With that said, Dick saw a slight glimmer of happiness on John's face.

There's something about knowing that everyone else is in the same sinking boat that makes you feel a lot better.

"John, I have a colleague who has a very unique view about all of this. She says there is a way for patients to find such answers about life by visiting their ancestors. Do you think that could help you?"

"You mean like a séance?"

"No. It's a form of psychotherapy involving altered states of consciousness."

"With drugs?"

"No. It's a process."

"Is it real?"

"What's real?" Dick didn't mean to be overly philosophical, but he wasn't sure how else to answer the question.

"Do you believe in it?" he asked Dick.

"I believe in her professionalism and she assures me that her patients' contacts with their ancestors are as real as you and I are sitting here right now."

John looked away for a minute as he considered the suggestion. "Why not?" he replied. "I've always wanted to know what happens."

***

CHAPTER 2
Other Realities

Their conversation had changed significantly with Joan discussing her experiences visiting primitive tribes in remote areas of the Amazon jungle. Early in the process, she told John he would have to accept some pretty weird phenomena if her methods were to help him.

"Jung explained that the collective unconscious includes spiritual glimpses into our ancestral life. That's where the archetypes of our myths and fairy tales reside."

"Witches, heroes and poems of the gods," Dick smiled.

"What you're saying is that you have some way for me to be magically transported back to the past."

"Sigmund Freud said, 'in the unconscious, nothing can be brought to an end, nothing is past or forgotten'."

"Like in our imaginations?" John asked.

"Or dreams," Dick said.

"In an altered state of consciousness you can connect with a distant relative, someone whom you've not met before. Consider the following. We think of time as linear. The apple hangs on the tree, then it falls to the ground, in a measurable quantity of time."

"Yeah, so." John said irreverently, still a little baffled by what she was talking about.

"If we change the way we think about time, our boundaries become limitless. You can travel to distant places just by touching different points on the great circle of time."

"If believing that time goes in a circle helps me understand what my life was all about, I'll do it."

Joan smiled as she handed John a small clay figure. "This is a goddess of Old Europe. She has the distended abdomen of pregnancy, our intimate connection with the cyclical nature of life."

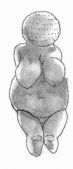

"Will I meet her?" he joked.

"Perhaps," Joan replied with a serious look. "Let's talk about you and this cycle. What do you observe about yourself as you sit here?" Joan asked.

"What do you mean?"

"Who is sitting there, thinking, talking, responding?"

"I am," John replied.

"Where does your voice come from?"

"My brain?" John shrugged.

She shook her head no, as that wasn't the answer. "You are thinking in linear time. Close your eyes and breathe deeply," she said. "Relax. Disconnect yourself from your body. Sense your being as a separate entity living within your body. When you're ready, quickly open your eyes and instantly twist your head to one side. Try to catch a glimpse of your soul."

John did just what Joan told him to. Dick did, too.

"Did you see it?" Joan asked.

"I think so. Just for a split second. As I opened my eyes, I could tell that there was something in me, separate from my body."

"For me, it's as if there's a benign freeloader residing inside me, not captured or trapped, but rather, for now, it's just in there. Maybe, it chose to be there or some force put it there," she said touching her heart. "Until it's time to move on."

"Death?"

"Death of this body, not my soul."

"So, having a soul implies there is life after death?" John asked.

"I think it anticipates some sort of continuation," she replied.

"My sense is that an element of one's past individuality can be found in your present soul. I'm sure that's what we all just caught a glimpse of," Dick added.

"But just a piece, though, right?" John wondered.

"Does it matter if it's just a part of it, John, and not all of it?" Joan asked.

"I guess not. At least then there's something beyond death," John concluded.

"Good," Joan added. "Now, I'd like to bring up one of my favorite books. It's called, The Tibetan Book of the Dead. Ever hear of it?"

"No," John squeaked out.

Joan and Dick knew that words like 'dead' were very charged for a patient in John's condition but they thought he could handle it.

"About seventy years ago we obtained the first translation of this ancient Tibetan Buddhist meditation on dying. Most people have no idea what happens when they die and they miss much of the experience. This text goes far beyond what's ordinary and you've already taken the first step toward understanding what's happening to you."

"I have?" John asked looking clearly puzzled by the conversation.

"Critical for karma are the events of birth and death. At these times, the soul is moving from the nontemporal to the temporal, or vice versa," Joan said.

"Vice Versa being my case."

"All of us die," Dick said.

"Those who follow this text are fond of quoting Abraham of Santa Clara," Joan added. "'He who dies before he dies, does not die when he dies.'"

"I like what Bob Dylan said better," John grinned. "'He not busy being born is busy dying.'"

"I like that, too," Joan beamed.

Dick just smiled, pleased at the progress John was making in accepting his fate.

***

"Aboriginal cultures don't differentiate between living and non-living as we do," Joan said.

"You mean dead or alive?"

"No, it's not about the fact that living things die, but rather that all things are alive, including for example rocks and water. Each living thing has its own attributes and capabilities, just as we humans have ours, but different."

"If you say so," John shrugged.

"The ancient people knew about the permanence of all existence and performed ceremonies using singing, dancing, rattling and drumming to get into a trance so they could communicate with different realities."

"What?"

"They could enter the world of spirits to get help to cure sickness or solve other problems, like a drought."

John looked doubtful as Joan continued to explain the strange revelations.

"You have already touched the edge of other realities."

"I have?"

"Like when you caught a glimpse of your soul."

"What do we do next?" he asked her.

"I'll show you." Joan took out a large drum from a bag that leaned against her chair. It was not the kind of drum most people have ever seen, but a simple flat wooden hoop, about a foot and a half in diameter, maybe four inches thick and covered on one side with a smooth skin.

"Bong." It made a hollow, deep resonating sound when Joan struck it with the padded stick. "Bong. Bong. Bong. Bong."

"John, lie on your back on the floor. Dick, please turn down the lights." They both did as she asked and waited in the darkness for her next instruction. "I want you to close your eyes, breathe deeply and relax. I'm going to play in a monotonous, repetitive way and all you have to do is focus on the sound. Okay?"

"What's going to happen?"

"We'll see."

"Bong. Bong. Bong. Bong. Bong. Bong. Bong. Bong."

***

"Did you hear that?" John asked in an excited voice.

"Hear what?" Joan and Dick replied simultaneously.

John hurried over to the window and, opening the shades with a burst of energy, looked out, expecting to see something other than cars going by on Memorial Drive. "It was the weirdest thing," he said, shaking his head as if he were crazy. "Did you hear it?"

"What?" they asked.

"The grunting noise. You must have."

"What happened?" Joan asked, winking to Dick that John's journey seemed to have been successful.

"I was standing in a pasture, all alone, when I suddenly heard a loud grunting noise and when I turned around, there was a huge buffalo standing not more than a few feet away. Before I knew it, a small calf came bounding up to me. I have no idea why I did this, but I reached out and grabbed the animal by its horns and we played tug of war." John looked at his hands as if he expected to see something on them. "The fur on its head was coarse and had bits of grass stuck in it."

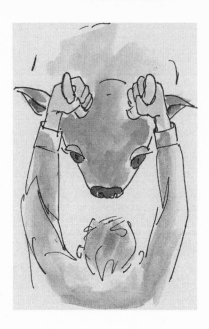

"How do you know the fur was coarse?" Joan asked.

"I felt it."

"Did they say anything to you?"

"No," he shook his head. "What does it mean?

"What do you think it means?"

"I had a dream about buffalos?"

"Were you sleeping?"

"No."

"Perhaps then it wasn't a dream." Dick said.

"I think you met your spirit helper," Joan added.

"My what?"

"Spirit helper. It can be a plant, animal, stone, or person. Your spirit guide chooses you and will help you journey to other worlds."

"I can't believe how real it seemed. I can still feel its hair between my fingers." John stared at Joan. "I wasn't dreaming? Maybe I'm just crazy."

"I don't think so. The sound of the drum transported you to an altered state." Joan replied. "At one time in our history, humans could talk to the animals and plants, possibly even to our gods."

"Maybe I should ask the buffalo to find a cure for my cancer."

"Perhaps," she acknowledged. "But I suspect the ancestors you meet will have some suggestions for you." She could tell by the look on his face that John was trying hard to accept what was happening. "Next time, I will teach you how to journey to what we call the upper and lower worlds. These are places you can visit and perhaps find some help."

"I could ask about the ultimate meaning of my life."

"You could," Dick said smiling, happy to hear that John was still intent on achieving his objective.

***

"When you were a kid, did you ever climb a tree?" Joan asked.

"There was a tree in the park near my house that I used to climb and pretend that the higher I went, the more invisible I became. I would climb up until I thought no one could see me."

"There are many versions of the astonishing tree that you'll climb now. It has exposed roots that are organized in such a manner that you can look far beyond where you are, deep down into the earth. If you climb in the other direction, you will reach heaven," Joan said, grinning at the mysterious splendor of her own remark.

"When do I leave?" John said with excitement in his voice.

"How about right now?" Joan replied and without delay she began to drum. "Bong. Bong. Bong. Bong."

***

"It would take fifty people holding hands to go around this tree," John drawled. He was in the beginning stages of a trance and in a few more minutes he would be transformed. "It's so tall I can't see the top," he continued, breathing with the beat of the drum. "The roots are tangled, but there is a space between them where I can climb down. I need to stretch as far as I can," and with that he drifted off into his journey.

John made his way down into the strangely bright darkness, following the roots until he came to the smooth hard bottom littered with small stones and bits of bark and leaves. He took several steps toward the dim light, finding the entrance to a cave that was partially blocked by the presence of a large rock. He climbed over it and continued on, negotiating around and over the rocks and stones that filled the narrow tunnel. After some time, John came to the exit and walked out into a green pasture growing under a sunny blue sky. On either side he could see the distant mountains and felt himself magically drawn into the knee-high grass that led toward what seemed an endless horizon far out in front of him.

"Grunt."

John jumped. Behind him stood the buffalo and her calf that he had met before. The calf was jumping up and down, signaling it wanted to play.

What happened next was most amazing, not that what had happened so far wasn't.

At the calf's encouragement, John flung himself onto her back, holding onto the horns with all his might. It was a good thing that he did, too, because the young buffalo immediately took off as if in a race and it was all he could do to hang on for dear life. As they flew higher, he could see a grove of trees straight ahead.

They touched down in a large field, but before he could get off she shook him to a thump onto the hard ground, right smack in the middle of a herd of buffalo. Then, walking in the direction of the trees, he noticed the closer he got to them, the wetter the once dry ground became. There must be a pond or stream nearby he thought, as he considered taking off his soggy socks to make walking a little easier.

"Bong. Bong. Bong. Bong."

It was the signal for him to go back. A shot ran through his heart when he realized the great tree was miles and miles away. "Where did they go?" he wondered now all alone. "How am I going to get back?"

It took John longer than he thought it should have, but he finally reached the tree as the drum continued to call him. He hurriedly scrambled and banged his way over the big rock at the entrance and quickly climbed up the roots.

"What happened?" Joan asked with a little worry in her voice.

His eyes came into focus in the dim yellow light of Dick's office. "Ouch! My knee," he exclaimed, pulling up his pants to reveal a fresh scrape. "On the way back, I was in a hurry and banged my knee on a large rock." Puzzled, he asked Joan and Dick how that could be, as he hadn't got up from the floor, much less left Dick's office. They told him that it was up to him to decide whether or not his experience was real or imaginary, but in any event, they assured him that he wasn't crazy.

Over the next few weeks, Joan worked with John as he journeyed numerous times to that place. Each time his experience was similar, but whenever he got close to the trees, the drum sounded, calling him back.

"Maybe, I'm afraid to find out what's in the grove of trees."

"What do you think is there?" Dick asked.

"I don't know." Then, becoming slightly pale, he stared at both his doctors and replied, "Maybe my death." He took several deep breaths, got up from the floor and gazed out the window at the clear night sky over the Charles River. "I guess I have to go there anyway, don't I?"

***

CHAPTER 3
The Grove of Trees

John maneuvered his way down through the tangled roots of the great sacred tree, carefully grasping smaller branches above his head while steadying his feet on larger ones below. In this manner, he squeezed his way along and, while holding on, felt the cool, smooth but noduled bark, getting some of it ground into the creases of his hands and fingers.

"Be careful," a root over his head said to him. "Hold on," warned another.

"Your name is John, isn't it?" said a polite voice.

"Yes."

"Do you know why you pass this way?"

"I'm not exactly sure," he replied.

"What we mean is, do you know where you're going?"

"I'm on my way to the grove of trees."

"We thought so," they mumbled.

"What do you know about the trees?" John asked them.

"We don't know very much," answered several. "We have never been that far, although we have discussed growing in that direction many times."

"We would like to know more," a deeper, older voice added.

"Perhaps the rocks and stones in the cave will have some information. They are closer to the trees and they may have even seen them or been otherwise informed," said another.

"Ask the rocks and stones," several roots said in unison.

"But please tell us about the trees when you return," they requested.

"I will," he called back.

John jumped down to the ground and quickly made his way into the cave.

"How do you talk to a rock?" he asked out loud, hoping they would hear him. But the rocks and stones were silent until he remembered what Joan had taught him about listening carefully.

"We don't know much about the grove of trees, either," a low voice said slowly.

"What? What did you say?" he yelled out.

"We can hear you better if you don't speak so rapidly," said one large stone.

"And please speak more softly," remarked another.

"We're not deaf, you know," said a third.

It seemed that John wasn't very good at talking to rocks and stones yet, so he listened some more.

"Sometimes, in the winter, the wind blows their leaves in here, but we really don't know them very well."

"Not many leaves get this far," said a large rock that he was just then crawling over.

It was remarkable, but as soon as he had let go of the ridiculous idea that roots couldn't talk and that rocks weren't alive he could hear them both speak. And, he noticed that the rocks and stones seemed to have a higher level of patience than the roots did, perhaps because the rocks and stones had been around so much longer.

"We expect that it will be a while before we are able to see the trees for ourselves, so we would like to hear your story about them, no matter how long it takes for you to come back this way," several rocks told John.

"It's the least I can do," he respectfully replied.

"We'll be waiting," they said.

***

No sooner had John grabbed two handfuls of coarse buffalo hair between his fingers, then the calf rocketed off across the great green plain, and the cool, fast wind instantly filled his eyes with tears. He was, however, still able to make out the distant grove of trees as they rapidly bounded along, propelled by the calf's feet that touched the ground just long enough to power them to an altitude of at least several hundred feet. Then, just as they were almost there, it was as if they had fallen right out of the sky and they came to a screeching stop on the slippery grass. John flew forward, flipped upside-down and ended up flat on his back with the calf standing over him and grinning broadly. By the time he got up and dusted himself off, his youthful traveling companion had vanished.

On his left, just several hundred yards away, was a very large pond surrounded by marsh grasses, with trees on the far side and that was perhaps half a mile away. There were a few people gathering something by the water and they looked over at him, but soon went back to work, seemingly untroubled by his presence in their land. The small stream of blue-gray smoke that rose in the distance signaled the presence of more people. Now, the gusty wind that had pushed them here from the west forced him to turn away, and it was then when he first noticed the small path trodden into the grass.

As he walked into their small village, the strangeness of the place should have suggested caution, though he only felt intrigued by what was before him. The houses were about ten by ten feet, and crudely assembled from trees into a shape similar to an American Indian teepee. The sticks did not meet at the top, but instead formed a small roof that was covered by sheaves of dried grass, save the hole for smoke to get out. Each house had an open doorway, about half his height, which faced out onto the pathway between the two rows.

The old woman sat on a wooden stool in front of her small house, seemingly unaware of his presence. A strange chill ran though his body and he jumped back when she looked his way, but he was relieved by the pleasant smile she gave him. She had been working on an article of clothing and after watching him for another moment, went back to her sewing.

Cautiously approaching her, he could see she was small and thin, and he immediately sat down on the ground close by, not wishing to intimidate her with his larger presence. She smiled again like she knew him, perhaps because his being there was expected and was no surprise to her. She was an older woman, sixty, seventy or more years of age, her brown hair now mostly gray, her hands and face weathered by time.

John watched as she used a stone knife to cut the hide she was working on. John noticed that the old woman had been observing him, too, and then suddenly she grinned again, revealing she had no teeth. It was, however, one of the kindest smiles that he had ever received and

John had no doubt that somehow she knew exactly who he was. Here was an opportunity to obtain information about the ultimate meaning of life, he thought, but then decided against mentioning it because how could she comprehend his impossible quest? But, what about his cancer? Maybe she would have a magical cure.

"John, I know that you have come here with important questions on your mind," she said, speaking first.

"What will happen to me?" he asked her.

He wasn't sure why he said that but it must have made sense because she seemed immediately concerned, yet she didn't reply. Instead, she pointed to the other villagers at their work tending fires, carving wood or grinding grain. They were going about their daily lives, seemingly without worry or apprehension and they didn't seem at all hurried, but nonetheless, one could tell they were diligent about their tasks.

"I need to know how you just accept your life," he asked the old woman. "Have you always lived like this? Don't you feel the need to change things?"

A flock of cackling geese flew over and took their attention. There were so many and they seemed so close to the ground, he felt as though he could reach out and grab one from the sky. The people at work looked to the geese, too, some going back to their chores right away, others staring dreamingly at their winged visitors. Why didn't they try to catch them, he thought.

"Just do it," the old woman said.

"Just do it? What do you mean?" John asked.

"It's easy," she smiled. "Just do it. It will be okay."

"It will be okay?"

"It will be okay," she smiled. "That's all there is."

"Bong. Bong. Bong. Bong. Bong. Bong. Bong. Bong."

The drum was calling him. He took one more hurried look at this old woman who was busy with her work. She knew exactly why he had come there and didn't need him to tell her about his divorce, job or even his cancer to understand what he was searching for. They were living precariously, thousands of years ago and didn't seem to have a care. They accepted life as it was, so why couldn't he?

***

John had drawn the pencil sketch of the village in perspective, with the old woman sitting on her stool by the nearest hut. Off to the right, in the distance, was the grove of birch trees. To the left he had drawn stands of marsh grasses growing along the edge of the large and flat pond that extended beyond view as it meandered through the grassy meadow.

"I could hardly believe my eyes," Joan said smiling, handing him a newspaper article about people who live in a remote village in Turkey. "When I saw this yesterday, it seemed as though it was from your journey."

What astonished her was the fact that John's drawing was almost exactly the same scene as the photograph in the article.

"What are you two looking at?" Dick asked, just about snatching the paper from John's hand.

"This village is like mine," John said staring at the photo.

"A coincidence?" Dick asked.

"I'm not sure it is just a coincidence," Joan said. "Your name is Holmes, correct?"

"Yes."

"Do you know what Holmes means in German or other Northern European languages?"

"No," John said with a puzzled expression.

"Holmes means a meadow land, near or surrounded by water and grassy plains."

John and Dick stared at Joan in disbelief.

"You're kidding," Dick finally got out.

John said nothing as he went over to the window and looked out onto the Charles River to see two boats racing each other to the Boston side.

"The name of my sailboat was Saxon. Years after I named it, I learned that my relatives lived in that part of Germany, before they migrated to England, a thousand years ago."

"From the Holmes Village," Dick suggested.

"So it seems," John replied.

"Who do you think the old woman was, or is, perhaps I should say?" Joan asked.

John looked out at the water again. "My great, great, great, whatever, grandmother."

"I think you're right," Joan replied.

"They're waiting for me, aren't they?" John asked us.

"Maybe," Dick said.

"Probably," Joan added.

"But she said that it would be okay," John protested.

"What do you think she meant?"

"When I'm dead I'll be with them and it will be okay."

"How do you feel about that?"

"Do you mean, how do I feel that I'll be dead like them or that I'll be dead and okay?"

"Either," Dick answered.

***

John began his next counseling session with an important announcement. "I've made a decision about my treatment options," he stated with confidence.

"Oh, good," Dick said immediately. "I think you made the right decision to start the treatments."

"I'm not going to get any," John stated, seeming genuinely relieved.

Both Joan and Dick were surprised though. "Have you told your doctors?" they asked.

"No, why should I?" John shrugged. "My cancer has progressed to a point where surgery and other treatments will not postpone my death. It's too late."

"I'm really sorry, John," Joan said.

"Don't be!" he exclaimed, standing up from the couch. "Look at me. Do I look sick? I don't feel sick."

"Are you sure about this, John?" Dick asked, very concerned for him.

"You know it wasn't a snap decision. We all die. We have established that fact. So, what's the point? I haven't missed anything in this life, and you said yourself it was a gift."

"You said that?" Joan questioned Dick with a frown.

"I did," Dick admitted.

"He was right," John offered in Dick's defense. "I can do anything I want for the next year or so and not be surprised when it all ends."

"What will you do?" Dick asked.

"I want to participate. I want to be involved."

"Ask them," Joan suggested.

"Ask who?"

"John, don't you see? You've met them. They know you. I'm sure they understand what's going on." John and Dick waited anxiously for her to continue. "I think you should go back there, to the Holmes village, and ask your great grandmother to introduce you to the village shaman. Perhaps, he will ask his spirit helpers to cure you."

"You really believe that would be possible?"

"Maybe." Joan could see that he hoped she was right. "Haven't you talked to roots and rocks and flown through the air on the back of a buffalo calf?" she asked John. "And, how long have humans been on this planet?" she asked Dick.

"Uh, fifty thousand years," Dick guessed.

"More. How long have we used radiation therapy and drugs to treat cancer?"

"Maybe fifty years."

"What did modern medicine offer before that?"

Dick was a little uncomfortable because he knew that the answer was almost nothing and he didn't want to say it because he thought it might pull the rug out from under John's hopes. Joan ignored Dick's hesitating.

"Nothing," she said, answering her own question. "How old would you say your great grandmother is?"

"She's older than I am," John replied.

"It's a widely held modern misconception that ancient man lived a short, brutish life. Just think about them taking all that time to make those wonderful cave paintings." Smiling at John, she continued. "John, you know first hand that ancient people lived just as long as we do and they didn't grovel about in the dirt just to stay alive. I believe their medicines worked well for them."

John nodded his tentative agreement but Dick still looked pretty doubtful.

"Joan, let's be realistic," Dick requested. "We don't want John to believe that some ancient medicine man will cure his cancer."

"John, Dick's got a point. There are no guarantees," she said.

"I know that."

"I'm not promising, I'm suggesting."

"I don't really care about getting cured. I'm excited because I think that old woman knows the true meaning of life. That's what I'm hoping to find out."

"Okay," Dick relinquished, "but I'm still a little doubtful about all of this."

"When do I go?" John asked.

***

The sound of the drum sent John scrambling down the tree roots, apologizing as he went because he hadn't told them about the birch trees and now he was in a big hurry to see his great great great grandmother again.

"We know, John," the roots said. "Just tell us everything when you come back."

"I promise I will." He meant it, too, he thought, as he crawled over the rocks towards the light ahead. He would tell them the story, too, on his way back.

"I came to ask you a question," he told the old woman, feeling uncomfortable because he was a stranger who might know her secrets. But her toothless smile comforted him and she said they had been waiting for his return. Then a man older than he was came over and sat down on the ground between them.

"I'm pleased to see that the Holmes family has done well," he said to John.

"What do you mean?"

"We are pleased to know that our family continues in your time."

"Are you my ancestor?" John asked.

"For more than two hundred generations."

"I'm sick, sir."

"We have been watching you," the man replied.

"You have?" Oh boy, John said to himself, a little ashamed about his less than perfect life. He wondered what this ancient man thought of him and his modern times, but they never got to that subject.

"Lie down. Let me look at you."

John obliged the man as though his request were nothing out of the ordinary and the man proceeded to glide a big goose tail feather a few inches over John's body. When the feather was near the area where the cancer was John thought he felt a strange tingling sensation.

Then, without indicating the basis for his next intentions, the man said, "I will be back in a little while," and walked away as calmly as he had arrived.

John leaned up on his elbows. "Who was he?" he asked the old woman.

"He is the grandfather of your grandfather's grandfather's grandfather, but longer ago than that."

"Oh," John said, and understanding now, but not knowing what else to say, he lay back down on the ground and watched her sew. Soon, he saw the great grandfather approach them and remarked that it was a quicker trip than he had anticipated, but the grandmother said the shaman had been gone for several days of John's time.

"They want you to visit with them and asked me to tell you," he informed John.

"Who are they?" John asked. "Are they my grandfathers too? How do I find them? Why do they want me to visit them?" John's head was swimming with questions and the old man knew John was anxious about what would happen, but this didn't change his deliberate peaceful demeanor.

"I will take you part of the way, as far as I am able," he paused. "They are the Old Ones."

"The Old Ones?" A chill ran up John's spine with that peculiar thought. He wasn't sure he wanted to meet people called the Old Ones. What would they do to him, he wondered?

"Do they know what's wrong with me?"

"They didn't tell me, but they have been expecting you."

The old grandmother was solemn, yet it didn't seem as though she was worried for John. "It will be okay," she told him several more times.

Before John could get the next question out of his mouth, the grandfather answered it.

"When you come back here, you will go to the Old Ones." There was some worry in John's face and the old grandfather saw it and tried to quiet his fears. "We will go together," he said quietly to John. "It will be okay."

***

"What did he say?" Dick asked.

"That I should get ready, and then come back and he would take me there, or at least part of the way to the Old Ones."

"Did he tell you where that was?"

"Did he say much about who you were going to meet?" Joan wanted to know.

"He just called them the Old Ones," John replied. "But I have to tell you that I have never, ever felt a chill like that before. When he said, the Old Ones. Wow!"

"The man you met was more than five thousand years old," Joan told them.

"He was?" John exclaimed, almost feeling that same chill again.

Joan said it was her best estimate based on the structure of the village and the tools they were using. "The Old Ones will be much older," she added.

"How old?" Dick asked.

"John, I think your great great grandfather is referring to Old Europe during the last Ice Age. About twenty thousand years ago."

"Whoa," Dick exclaimed. "How do you know that, Joan?"

"She met the Old Ones in her journeys," John kidded.

"No, but I know someone who might have."

John and Dick looked at one another in mutual disbelief.

"Who?" John asked.

"While I was studying in Europe, I became very good friends with a fellow graduate student, Marlise Pomard. She is now one of the world's foremost experts in Paleolithic cave paintings. She is also a student of shamanism. I would like you to meet her." John's puzzled look told Joan that he wasn't sure where this conversation was going, so she clarified her intentions. "With your permission, I would like to tell her about you and request that you go to France to continue this work."

"France?"

"She is a wonderful person, and I'm sure she will agree."

"Sounds like an appropriate next step," Dick suggested.

"Okay," John said with some hesitation. "But first, I'm going to look up an old friend who lives in Paris and go out on the town."

"If you do," Dick admonished, "take care of yourself."

"Or else, what, I'll?"

"Don't say it," Joan and Dick said at once.

"I'll be okay, remember?" John said, continuing to smile. He was excited about seeing Henri again and said he was also looking forward to the sessions with Marlise.

Joan called France that evening, even though it was past midnight there, to let Marlise know that John was ready.

**

CHAPTER 4
John's Dear Friend, Henri

Joan instructed that he make arrangements to meet Marlise Pomard two weeks from then, in the Dordogne region of France.

"Good, because I already told Henri I would be coming," John admitted.

"Who is this Henri fellow, anyway?" Dick wanted to know.

"My friend Henri Honoré is a famous abstract artist. If you visit him at his gallery in Paris, anytime, you'll find him surrounded by students and wealthy patrons."

"How do you know him?" Joan asked.

"We met on a train. We were both going to Lyon and we just started talking. Before we got there, we had become great friends," John smiled as he remembered that trip.

"When was that?" Dick asked.

"About twenty-five years ago."

"That's quite a friendship."

"It's wonderful that the two of you still stay in touch," Joan mused. "I'll bet you and Marlise hit if off right away, too."

"He's getting old now. He was a young man during the war and I'm looking forward to spending some time with him. Before we're both dead."

"John." Joan said his name with an inflection of sorrow, but also was suggesting that he shouldn't be feeling sorry for himself. It wouldn't help.

"I have something for you," Dick said, handing John a large book.

"Prehistoric Artists in France," John said, opening it randomly. "Venus a la Corne, from a rock shelter in Laussel, France. Another fat and pregnant cavewoman," he grinned. "Does this mean I'm going to meet one?"

"Perhaps," she smiled. "These figures were made to capture the miracle of birth and symbolize the renewal of life," she said. "You know, the great cycle we all find ourselves in."

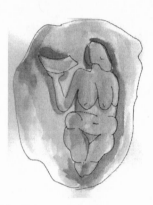

John flipped through a few more pages then closed the book, trying not to look as gloomy as he felt. "Thanks," he said to both of them.

***

As the Air France jet maneuvered its way to the terminal, John tried to rub his bleary eyes awake. He hadn't slept much on the flight from Boston because the discussion he had had with Joan and Dick kept waking him up over the middle of the Atlantic. She had said that it was not just all in his head, but Dick had counseled that it could be. But he had heard the snort, felt the coarse buffalo hair between his fingers and scraped his knee, all while he lay on the floor in Dick's office. Joan was convinced that he had achieved the required ecstatic state of consciousness to travel down the roots, through the cave of talking rocks, and then on to meet with the old grandmother and grandfather in their dimension of time. Even Dick couldn't reconcile why John's drawing of the Holmes village was so similar to the newspaper photo.

Marlise would instruct him further in the substance and technique of the ancient shamanic trance and then they would explore the prehistoric carvings and paintings of the Dordogne region. Joan believed this was the time period of the Old Ones and she argued that the paintings in the French caves were made during shamanic journeys. As the ancient participants went deeper and deeper into their magical transformations, the parietal surfaces would become animated with the curved shapes and wavy lines that drew them further into the vortex of the spirit world. The shaman would become part man, part animal, but retain sufficient human awareness so he could retrieve a cure from the gods. Marlise was to help John make his journey to the Old Ones so he could find out why they wanted to see him. Perhaps, they would cure his cancer or even share their insight into the ultimate meaning of his life.

The door to the Airbus opened and John stumbled out into the morning bustle of Charles de Gaulle Airport, hoping that the trip into Paris would be quick. He would try to sleep for only a few hours and adjust to this time zone. Then he would stay up all night with his friend Henri.

***

"John?" the voice on the telephone said.

"Henri! Bonjour," John replied with enthusiasm, trying to disguise that the telephone had just awakened him.

"How are you doing, John?"

"Ca va bien."

"Good." Henri paused for a moment. "Are you ready? It's five."

"Five! I've slept all day?"

"I've done it myself," Henri laughed. "Take your time, I'll be waiting."

"I'll be down in ten."

"Good to hear your voice again, John."

John hung up. "I guess now I'm rested enough to stay up all night."

***

The elevator door opened and his old friend stood across the hall. "Henri," John said extending his hand, but Henri put his arms around John instead.

"It's really great to see you."

"You too, mon ami," John replied.

"Are you ready for Paris?"

"I can't wait. Let's walk down Boulevard Montparnasse to my favorite restaurant, okay?"

It was about fifteen minutes to Le Perfect and, as they dodged all the people in their path, they had a chance to catch up and remember their last time together in Paris. It was a great reunion for the two old friends.

"What have you been doing with yourself, John?"

"I got divorced. Then I got fired."

"Which did you prefer?" joked the Frenchman.

"It was a toss up," John chuckled.

They both laughed some more then John went on to tell Henri about the winding down of his personal and professional lives. Henri was older than John and had been through both situations on at least several occasions, so he had no problem reassuring his younger colleague that it didn't mean much and all was for the best.

Henri pulled open the restaurant door and they went into the clamor and out of the streetlights of Paris on that chilly, late fall evening.

"Bonsoir."

"Bonsoir," Henri and John responded in unison to the maitre'd.

"Deux?"

"Oui."

He gave them a pleasant table by the window, opposite the bar, but far enough away to be private. In ancient ritual, they clinked their glasses to their long friendship and lives of traveling the world.

"It's good to have that all behind you," Henri said, studying his friend over the rim of his glass. "Isn't it?"

"Yeah, things don't have to last forever to be worthwhile."

Henri grinned. "That line won't work on me."

"It won't?" John grinned. "I guess I got burned out."

"You got bored."

Henri took another sip of his drink and, after fidgeting his glass into its original place on the crisp white tablecloth, gave John a look that betrayed his sorrow. "How much time do you have?"

"I have to leave Paris the day after tomorrow."

"That's not what I mean."

John looked to his friend and admitted the truth. "I guess I have a year."

"Why didn't you call me?"

"I just found out."

Henri sighed as John tried to smile away the melancholy they both felt for the friendship they would both soon loose.

"They can't fix it?"

John shook his head no. He glanced out to the Parisian sidewalk but it didn't keep his attention like the sailboats on the Charles River.

"Je t'aime," Henri told him.

"I love you, too, Henri."

***

They strolled though the back streets of Montparnasse, slowly making their way to their favorite late night bar, The Rose, to have another drink or two.

"Isn't this the famous Cimetiere du Montparnasse?" John queried of his good friend.

"It is," Henri replied with some hesitation.

"Let's go in," John suggested.

"You sure?"

"I've walked by many times, but have never been inside."

"Perhaps, it's not open so late," protested Henri.

"Then we'll go American style and hop the fence."

They went into the crowded place that was lit only by the yellow haze of streetlights, staying close together as they walked up and down the cobble stone paths, giving only cursory examinations to the gravestones.

"I've become comfortable with my death, Henri." John told him that his therapist had suggested knowing when you were going to die was a gift in disguise, but Henri remained silent as he listened to his friend. "Or else I wouldn't be here with you now."

Henri stopped. "Look here," he pointed. "We're in luck."

"Jean-Paul Sartre. 1905 to 1980," John read.

"I remember when he died. Fifty thousand people, including me, attended his funeral."

"The father of existentialism," John remarked. "But some of them, like Kierkegaard, were so depressing."

"This is the story of the Danes, not the French," Henri chuckled. "We French know how to live."

"That's why I'm in Paris."

"You know that Sartre was an atheist."

John didn't respond as they walked along in silence toward the exit.

"Though at the end of his life, he seemed to struggle with it. He may have even expressed a belief in God in his last writings," Henri added.

"Interesting. Let's go get a drink and I'll tell you what I'm going to do," John said.

***

It was one-thirty in the morning and The Rose was packed to the gills with locals, making it necessary for them to patiently squeeze their way between the conversations and Gauloises to get to the bar.

"I don't know what to say, John."

"You don't have to say anything. We're friends, remember?"

Henri smiled and patted him on the back. "What's this special thing you wanted to tell me?"

They both took a drink and John spoke over the noise. "Do you know what a shaman is?"

"I do," he said. "Have you found one to cure you?" Henri smiled a little.

"Maybe. My shrink brought an anthropologist into my sessions and she showed me how to travel back in time."

"I know about this," Henri acknowledged.

John then told him about the sacred world tree, the talking roots and all the other things he had recently experienced, including his visit to the Holmes site. Henri was amazed by the story about the newspaper article, as well as the translation of John's German surname.

"So, you are a warrior from the North, visiting us here in the romantic South. What's next for you?" Henri kidded.

"I'm going to meet a colleague of Joan's. She's an expert in cave paintings."

"I have been to Lascaux, the original one, while it was still open to the public. It is fantastic."

John explained the possible link between the paintings and the Old Ones he would try to meet with.

"Did you say Marlise Pomard?"

"I did. Why?"

"She is from the Sorbonne and a very famous scientist. You're going to meet with her?"

"Did you think I came here just to see you?"

Henri laughed and clinked his glass into John's. "To the Old Ones," he smiled.

***

It was late evening, two days later, when John arrived in Perigeux. In the almost silent darkness of the station he wondered how long he would be there, or for that matter, what would happen to him by the end of the next day. It was Joan who had made the formal arrangements and he had received only a short note from the telephone operator at his hotel in Paris that Dr. Pomard was expecting him in Periguex. He was intrigued about what she would be like, but for tonight he hoped he would be able to go to sleep and forget about how much he already missed his dear friend, Henri.

***

CHAPTER 5
La Boulangerie

J e voudrais un café, s'il vous plaît," John said to the waitress in his best French accent.

"Would you like something to eat as well, Monsieur?"

"Yes, please. I would like a croissant."

"They're perfect today," she said with a little grin.

He started to gaze out the window, but instead called out to her across the café. "Deux, please. I'm hungry."

It was a great little place and probably hadn't changed a bit since the war, he daydreamed out the window wishing, too, he had known a long time ago how truly pleasant it would be.

"Would you like some more coffee?"

He nodded with a smile. "Do you know a Dr. Pomard? I'm to meet her here this morning?"

"Oui. You will have no trouble recognizing her," the waitress replied. So, the instructions had been correct. He would wait for the woman and drink his coffee, savoring the moments in this perfect French country boulangerie.

She interrupted his thoughts when she sat down and took a big, noisy sip of the coffee she had brought over for herself. She was a little younger than he was, and quintessentially French; petite, with short, light brown hair, and her nose was a little too long but not at all unattractive. He liked the way she appeared and was just going to say something when she spoke.

"Did you have a pleasant journey to Perigeux?"

"Uh, yes, I did," he replied, admitting the obvious. "I was fortunate to travel as far as Tours with an old friend."

"Was that Henri?" she asked.

How could she know that he wondered. "Dr. Pomard?"

"Oui, I am Marlise Pomard," she grinned.

"You work here, in a bakery?" It was a silly thing to say, but it was the best he could do, taken by surprise like that.

"I love the smell of fresh bread in the early morning. This is my family's boulangerie and I help them out sometimes, mostly so I can eat some," she said grinning even more. "I thought this would be a good place to talk, okay?"

"Sure, why not?" John replied, smiling too. "You knew who I was all along, didn't you?"

"Yes, of course, but I still had my apron on when you came in, so I thought I would play a little game. It's in my French nature. You're not upset, are you?"

"To the contrary, I have found our discussions quite appealing so far. It's as if I have already met two nice French women this morning." Joan had been correct; they would hit it off right away.

"We have a lot of work to do," she said, half smiling, half professional.

"What has Joan told you?"

"Everything."

"Then you know I'm dying."

Her professional demeanor then took over. "Do I need to know anything? I mean, from a medical perspective?"

"I'm okay for now. I'm just dying," John said. "You could get me another croissant quickly though," he added, smiling as he kidded her.

They both laughed again and then began the discussion John had come there to have. She was fascinated by the stories about the visits with his ancestors and it was making sense why Joan had wanted him to come to France and work with her. She, too, had been working to contact the Old Ones but had never been personally invited, as he had been, to visit them. Her proposal was they make a shamanic journey to the Holmes village together and ask to be guided to the Old Ones. She hoped her long-standing spiritual connections to the people who originally made the cave paintings on her family's property would provide a rationale for her participation. Marlise was honest with John about her hopes for this most cherished of scientific objectives, but she also was quite clear that she expected to focus her efforts primarily on his search for the ultimate meaning of his life.

"Do you think the Old Ones can cure my cancer?" he asked her somewhat reluctantly.

"I believe that the shamans once visited the gods to find cures. I'm just not sure if the Old Ones will be able to help you or not," she stressed. "But, whether they do or not, you must see the exceptional adventure in all of this?"

"I do," he replied with renewed energy. "When do we go?"

She glanced outside. "Let's stretch our legs first. It looks like it's becoming a nice day."

***

They crossed the street to avoid the tables on the sidewalk and, as they sauntered along, Marlise gave him a brief course in Paleolithic art history, discussing the ancient Mousterian, then the Aurignacian, Gravettian, and finally the Solutrean and Magdalenian, the last two time periods the ones they planned to travel to. On the way back to her boulangerie, she somewhat matter-of-factly gave John the small, stone figure.

"I've seen these before," he remarked, stopping to examine the object.

"You have?"

"Joan."

"Good. This one's a copy of a famous Venus carving found nearby."

"I like it."

"I made it myself."

"You did? Is it magic?" he asked with all seriousness.

"It hasn't been for me, but maybe for you," Marlise replied.

It was a very well executed piece and he told her so as he handed it back.

"It's for you," she told him.

"It is?"

"Oui."

"Merci beaucoup," he replied, carefully putting the object into his jacket pocket.

"Today, we call this 'art moblier'," she smiled.

"Portable art."

"Oui. We admire the artistic style and think that it is beautiful, which it is. More importantly, these pieces were once a part of everyday life, yet integral to spiritual life."

"Everyday life?"

"In that long ago time, there was no difference between the sacred and the profane. Just as for the cave paintings, it is actual, not symbolic, life. Why else would you be able to talk directly to your gods?" she asked with all seriousness.

"Only in the Garden of Eden?"

"Exactly."

They walked along while Marlise did her best to describe the incredible mystical beauty of the paintings at famous sites such as Niaux, Trois-Freres and Lascaux. She promised to take him to some, too, if they had time. Mostly, their work would be at the cave located on her family's property and which she was authorized by the government to use.

"Scientific purposes. Is that what we're doing?"

Marlise smiled at John. She put a friendly arm into his, the one in the pocket that held the stone Venus figurine. "Something like that," she smiled again. "I think it's time for coffee."

"Okay," John replied, wondering what was next.

***

She pulled the old blue Fiat up to the side of the petite stone house and waited as John caught up to her on the other side of the car. She walked ahead on the path into the woods and John followed. Occasionally, there were glimpses to be caught of ancient limestone walls that followed along the river.

"Help me, please," she asked, and John grabbed the branches from her. Marlise kneeled down and immediately began to crawl into the one meter wide opening. "Be careful not to hit your head," she warned.

John moved his way past the bush and followed her into the chalky roughness of the cave. The earth was cool on his hands, quite damp he thought, although he couldn't be sure because it was so dark. He wondered what he was doing there and was just considering that this woman could be leading him into some sort of trouble when Marlise interrupted his silent concerns.

"Don't worry, John. We'll be there in a few more minutes." Somehow she knew what he had been thinking.

They emerged into a small room lit by a sliver of sunshine that filtered through a small crack in the stone ceiling. The cave was just tall enough to sit up in and she motioned for him to come over next to her.

"Close your eyes and hold my hands. Take a deep breath and let out all the tension you have inside." He did as she instructed and to his surprise, felt better immediately.

"Are you okay, now?"

"I can hear a noise. What is it?" he asked her.

"Listen carefully," she instructed.

It was the beating of his own heart that he heard thumping in his ears.

"It's a kind of womb we're in, isn't it?"

"Oui," she replied. "Are you ready to go on?" He let her know he was by squeezing her hand a little. "We're going to go through another passageway and then we'll come to a place where we can stand up and you'll see the carvings," she said.

They made their way into the next opening, crawling on their hands and knees in the cool darkness.

"We need to lie down here," she called back, and for the next few meters they moved forward on their bellies.

"I'm all right," he volunteered. "I'm getting used to the darkness." In front of him he saw a strange, human-like form but it turned out to be Marlise standing up, shining a small flashlight.

"Look at the wall," she said, illuminating what seemed to be scratches into the rock. There were carved squares and several lines of holes, about five millimeters in diameter, which looked as though they had been just recently poked into the rock.

"They were made at a time when the rock was soft, perhaps with a stick from the same bush that now guards the entrance, maybe twenty thousand years ago."

"What do they mean?"

"The squares are female, the holes, male. Together, they are the dynamic balance of nature. They were made by people recalling the beginning stages of their shamanic journeys."

"Altered states of consciousness?"

"Oui."

"I have seen strange lines in the air, too, flying about, as I climbed down the roots, on my way to the Holmes village."

"These shapes are the same phenomenon. It is like this for me, too."

"Then I'm not crazy, am I?"

"Perhaps we both are," she laughed.

"The second of the three phases of the shamanic trance is often drawn as a transition, such as when geometrics are combined with animal figures," Marlise explained, shining the light to the dark side of the cave and onto a hole in the wall that was less than a meter in diameter. "We will go through there to get to the next chamber. It's a short way, but very tight and it goes downhill, so you will feel like you are falling. Ready?"

"I can't go back now."

After several more minutes they emerged into a small, irregularly shaped cave that was almost, but not quite, high enough to stand up in. The ceiling was fairly smooth and covered with carvings of bison, prehistoric deer and horses. Marlise was careful not to touch the fragile surfaces as she pointed out the wavy lines and contorted figures.

"We are deep inside the cave now and the Old Ones are remembering the strange sensations of leaving behind any recollection of normal consciousness as they enter the world of the, the."

"The gods?"

"I think so. It is a situation with which we are no longer familiar. We humans are gone now from the sacred."

"Regrettably," John added.

"The next cave is the most astonishing of all, and it is the kind of place where I expect we may meet the Old Ones. I will show you this cave now, so later you will remember how it feels in there." She was silent for a moment and he held all his questions, waiting for her. "John," she continued, "I must admit to you that although I have been in that cave many times, I have never been there on a shamanic journey. I have no idea what we will find when we are in a trance and find the Old Ones."

"What do I do?"

"The cave is about ten meters through that tunnel. Take a look around and orient yourself. Then I'll turn off the flashlight. We need to take off our clothes so we don't bring any more modern contaminants into the cave than absolutely necessary."

When they came out on the other side of the tunnel, Marlise held her hand over the flashlight, allowing just enough light to escape so they could see the paintings. Bison, ibex, deer, spotted horses. The colors were magnificent hues of red and yellow ochres, and the pigments represented ever-lasting life, she said.

"John, look at that one."

"It's a lion."

"Look more closely."

Deep inside a small dark cave, somewhere in the middle of France, he was staring at a lion-man painted on a ceiling thousands years ago by a human who had stood in exactly the same spot where he was now was, and a powerful chill tingled throughout his body and it wouldn't leave him.

***

CHAPTER 6
The Old Ones

Marlise asked John to hold the wooden hoop and help her stretch the freshly washed raw goat's skin over it. It was like slippery wet rubber and John struggled a bit to keep the hide in place as Marlise fastened it.

"I like the sound of these drums," John said.

"Humans have made them for more than twenty thousand years."

"For the purposes of inducing a trance?"

"Oui," she nodded. "But, they don't work for us as well as they once did."

"What do you mean?"

"Our overly analytical manner of thinking has caused us to lose our direct connection to the gods."

"We got kicked out of the Garden of Eden?"

"Oui. We got too big for our britches and opened Pandora's box," she smiled, examining the new drum. "As it dries, we carefully twist the hide strips to obtain the proper tension."

"What was the alternative?"

"I don't know. Maybe, there was no choice. It's earth's first experiment with humans. But, we don't really get it, not until we face our death," she cringed, immediately realizing the insensitivity of her remark. Marlise tried to apologize.

"But, you're right," John stressed. "I didn't really try to understand the meaning of my life until I found out I was going to die."

"It's going to be a good drum, you know. And you will be the first to play it," she promised. "Together, we will climb down the tree and make our way from the cave to the village."

"The landmarks are very clear," John added.

"Are you remembering them now?" she asked, looking into his faraway eyes.

"Yes," he nodded. "I am."

"This drum will send us there," she smiled.

"I find this all quite remarkable, don't you?"

Marlise didn't answer except with a smile.

While the drum dried, they spent the next several days with John telling her everything about himself that could be important to their journey and, as they prepared for what would come next, they became good friends.

***

It was the same for John as it had been each time he climbed down the tangle of roots, except today they wanted to know about his friend.

"My name is Marlise Pomard," she replied to the roots.

"We know who you are," said the roots in the immediate vicinity. "But, why are you here with John?"

"He is taking me to the Holmes village, to visit his ancestors."

"Oh," they exclaimed in unison. One could tell by their tone that they were curious and very excited as well. "By the way, John, you promised the last time you were here you would tell us about the village. You know that we're not trying to pry into your life, but because we have never been there ourselves, we are very interested in what it looks like and who lives there."

"I'm sorry I haven't taken the time. It seems I'm always in a hurry to get back."

"That's what they all say. You should know by now, John, that there is no such thing as time, so there's no reason to be in a hurry."

"I'm beginning to understand that."

"Well, take our word for it. We can't even remember where we were before we were here. And the stones told us that they have always been here."

"So, maybe time does exist. Perhaps something can continue for so long that we simply forget?" Marlise asked the roots.

There was a long silence and then some unintelligible mumbling before the roots replied. "You're a philosopher, correct?"

"No. Actually, I'm an anthropologist."

"Well, okay, then. But, please be sure to remind John to tell us about the village when you come back this way. We really would like to know about it. And he promised us."

John jumped from the lowest root onto the floor of the cave then reached back to help Marlise. As she let go of the roots, she glanced back at them.

"You have all been very kind to let us climb down. I'll make sure that John tells you about our journey."

"She is a very nice a person, don't you think?" the roots remarked.

***

Marlise and John had a similar conversation with the stones as they crawled over them toward the light coming into the cave. They committed to one another to spend time with both the roots and the stones when they returned, agreeing that there was no reason to be in a hurry.

"Who is this?" the buffalo calf asked, standing back as John and Marlise emerged from the cave.

"I am Marlise Pomard and I'm traveling to the Holmes village with John. Then we are on our way to visit the Old Ones."

"I knew that," smiled the calf. "But I wanted to make sure that you knew who you really are," the buffalo calf said, her eyes twinkling in the bright sunlight. "What are you waiting for? Get on and I will take you as far as I can."

Marlise was glad that John had forewarned her about this part of the journey and she had grabbed two handfuls of buffalo hair just in time as they took off into the cool wind. He had, however, not sufficiently prepared her for the abruptness of the landing that would fling them both to the ground. John later agreed with Marlise that the calf probably enjoyed throwing her passengers high into the air and deliberately thumping them down onto the grassy plain.

The village appeared exactly as John had said it would and even from where they had landed Marlise could make out John's ancient grandmother sitting by the door to her small house.

"It's nice to see you again, grandmother."

Her toothless smile immediately endeared her to Marlise as it had for John.

"Walk there," she said, pointing to the other end of the village. "He's been waiting for you."

They said goodbye and went the short distance to the man sitting on the ground, and in the process passing by the small huts that made up the village. Everyone acknowledged them with a polite nod or a smile as they went by.

"This place is absolutely marvelous, John." It was a very small village Marlise thought, but more scientifically exhilarating than any anthropologist could have ever believed possible.

"I told you so," John said.

"I can't believe it's still here, after all this time."

"Time?" he smiled.

"You know what I mean."

They sat down next to the grandfather who had remained motionless, his legs crossed and eyes tightly closed. It seemed as though he might be asleep and they told each other with silent glances to be quiet and wait for him to wake up.

"I know you," he said, startling them both. "I have met your grandfather," he added while opening his eyes at Marlise. "He lives not far from here. He told me that you would be coming here with John."

"Oh, my God," she said, stunned and clutching at her heart.

The man did not move but glanced a greeting into John's eyes.

"Can I, I mean, will you show me the way? To my grandfather," she asked.

His eyes softened and he spoke to her with an easy kindness in his voice. "Oui, mais pas maintenant. Vous reviendrez ici autrefois et je vous prendrai pour le voir."

"Merci," she replied with a big sigh. "Merci grand-pere beaucoup grand."

"I am ready to take you to the Old Ones" he said, and immediately he got up and started for the nearby trees. John and Marlise scrambled to their feet and caught up to him, staying close behind for fear they would get lost in the thick birch.

"What did he say to you, Marlise?" John asked.

"He told me to come back and he would take me to visit with my great, great grandfather."

John noticed that tears had filled her eyes.

"This is really happening, isn't it?"

"Oui," she choked a little.

***

After what seemed to be at least an hour of walking, the old grandfather abruptly stopped and quieted himself to their surroundings. He carefully examined the woods then raised his arms up to the sky before moving the branches of the bush aside.

"How did we get here?" John asked Marlise, recognizing that they had come to the cave on her family's property in the Dordogne. This was quite strange, as they had arrived here by a very different route. Marlise didn't seem to care, or even to notice this and she ignored John's question as she went up to the hole in the limestone and peered in.

His grandfather motioned to him, taking John by the arm and pulling him close. "Ce que Dieu garde, est bein garde," he whispered, then moved away so John could follow Marlise into the cave.

The two of them clamored into the alkaline smell of that familiar cool, damp place and in a minute or so they were within the short closeness of the first cave.

"Are you all right?" she asked.

John took several deep breaths and said that he was. "What did he say to me?"

"It is an old French proverb, obviously much older than I thought it was. It means, 'they whom God takes care of, are in safe protection.'"

"God! He said God?"

"Oui. It seems God has been with us for a very long time."

He stared at her in the darkness. "Are we in danger, Marlise?"

"I'm not sure," she said, pausing for a moment. "Can I be totally honest with you, John?"

"Please do, before I explode with anticipation."

"What's the worst that can happen?"

"We could die," John replied.

"I think so, too," Marlise agreed.

"Are you okay with that? I mean I'm the one that's dying soon, not you," he asked.

"Oui, but we are all dying. I'm so intrigued I must go on. We are so close to the Old Ones. No one has ever come so far."

They crawled through the next passageway to the cave of geometric carvings and further transition, then going into the last, small dark tunnel. They were now far beyond any awareness of ordinary consciousness. They thought the pounding they heard came from their hearts, but it was from the last cave. In the yellowish darkness, they removed their clothes and crawled on their bellies into the final passageway, now only a few meters away from the Old Ones.

***

His old grandfather's words hung in his mind. Was it a warning of an instant demise or a blessing? In the dim light made by stone bowls burning animal fat, they could make out a small child, perhaps five years old, banging on the skull of a bear. It sounded a lot like the drum they had constructed in Marlise's kitchen, the one that had brought them here, and the deep mellow resonance relaxed him, right up to the moment the child's eyes met his. As it turned out, the Old Ones had already discovered their presence.

"Sit there," the man closest to the passageway said to them, pointing to a space near the fire.

"These are for you," a youthful woman said as she came over to where John and Marlise huddled together. She handed them each a large hide cover then scrambled into the passageway at the sound of distant voices, leaving them wondering what would happen next.

"I am Dag," a large, middle-aged man said coming out of the tunnel. Then paying them no more attention, he embraced his brother Lug, as the people of the cave gathered around the fire to welcome those returning from their travels and the young woman called Nu motioned for John and Marlise to join their reunion.

***

Dag handed Lug a fist-sized rock then sat there looking pleased with himself while his brother closely examined the ordinary-looking thing, which included touching the stone with his tongue in several places, something John thought a little strange.

"It's flint," Marlise whispered to John. "To make knife blades and scrappers."

Lug abruptly glanced over to John so as to get his attention, and then as John watched, used a hammerstone to neatly cleave off a large slice of flint from the core. He handed the piece to John, who, to everyone's instant amusement, managed to cut his finger while studying the sharp, fresh blade.

It was during the ensuing discussion about Dag's long trek to the flint mines that John decided to return the present by giving Lug the Venus figurine Marlise had given him.

"This is for you," John said, handing the stone carving to a very surprised Lug who immediately held the sacred object over his head for all to see. There was no mistaking his instant admiration for John. Another man brought over a small hide packet and rattled over it with some small bones tied together by thin hide strips. Lug carefully opened the case and picked out another stone carving. It, too, was a pregnant Venus figurine and Lug held one in each hand, motioning for Nu to come closer so he could put them against her bosom.

Lug slid closer to John and Marlise and put his arms around them both. In that extraordinary moment occurred an indisputable physical contact between an Ice Age man and his twenty-first century visitors. The act was as real as the buffalo grunt or handful of buffalo hair grabbed during flight. It was as genuine as the scrape on John's knee or his more recent cut from the razor-sharp stone sliver.

John smiled at everyone in the cave as Marlise looked on with tears of wonder streaming down her face.

***

"How long have you been here?" John asked them.

"We have always been here," Lyon replied from his seat near the fire. He wore a skin just like the ones that had been given to John and Marlise and his head was adorned with the skull of a male lion that still retained the fangs and the animal's long mane now flowed down his back.

"It's lion, isn't it?" John asked.

Lyon touched the skin he wore then pointed to John's. "Yes, that's what I mean," John indicated.

"We are the lion people," he nodded. "Where are you from?" Lyon asked.

John and Marlise searched each other's face, but quickly realized how very complicated it would be to explain the modern world to these ancient people.

"We came from the Holmes village," John announced in a clear, forthright voice.

The men glanced around their circle and he could tell by their expressions that they understood and were satisfied with his reply. They wouldn't want to hear about modern civilization anyway.

"Your grandfather talked to us in his dreams. He told us you were sick and we answered that he show you the way here," Lug revealed.

Dag held out his hands and John took hold of them. "You are of us," he said to John. "As is the old man in the village," he said smiling broadly.

Nearby, Lyon rattled his bones and John began to feel very strange indeed. He soon began to vibrate all over, so much so that Marlise had to put her arms around him, but John loosened in her grip and collapsed to the cave floor, transported into an even deeper trance by Lyon's rattling and chanting.

The men moved John closer to the fire, carefully placing him on his back in the middle of a great lion skin, uncovering him and trusting the fire to heat his naked form inside the cool cave. Marlise moved back toward a wall as Lyon and another man emerged from the shadows of the cave, both of them wearing lion skull headdresses, Lyon with two rattles and the other man beating on a bear skull drum. She saw Lug and Dag's approach to John by their shadows on the walls of the cave. They, too, wore the skull of a lion and beat their drums in rhythm. The four men kneeled closely around John, drumming and rattling with such intensity and loudness that Marlise was forced to cover her head with the lion skin, thinking the noise would drive her mad.

"Roarrrr!"

Marlise was scared to death and wouldn't peak out from under her blanket for fear of seeing whatever creature made that horrific sound.

"Roarrrr! Roarrrr!"

Marlise quivered under the covers until she fell asleep. When she awoke, it was so quiet it seemed as though everyone must have run out of the cave to save themselves and hadn't noticed her slumped over in the darkness. My God, she wondered, what's happened to John? Then she heard the footsteps. Something was walking around in the cave. She took a deep breath and forced herself to peek out, half expecting that she would be eaten alive. What she saw was even more terrifying.

Moving slowly around John's still body were four huge lions. They clawed the ground as they paced, making advances toward John with their open mouths, growling, as if they were going to attack him. She forgot the fear she felt for herself and began to pray out loud that John would be killed quickly and not suffer the excruciating pain she imagined would next be hers. Then, without further warning, one of the lions bit into John's abdomen and, jerking his mighty head back, pulled out some of John's insides. The lion chewed for a moment then went back for another bite, the other three carnivores patiently waiting for their leader to get his fill. The lion took another large bite of John and then, in a single leap, jumped from the fire to where Marlise hid.

"Roarrrr!" said the lion violently, causing her to faint that instant.

***

Marlise had no idea how long she had been out when she awoke to soft voices and a residual of the fear that had kept her eyes so tightly closed. Outside her covers, it would be either Heaven or Hell she decided.

"Marlise. Marlise," she heard John say. "You okay?"

She felt his hand shake her and saw he was lying on the ground next to her, partly covered by a lion skin.

"You're not dead, are you?" she asked in her confusion.

"Not unless we both are," he smiled, patting her arm.

She looked around the cave and saw the Old Ones going about their typical activities. "What happened?" she asked.

"Lyon cured me," he replied.

"Cured?"

John nodded. "He said the disease came from where I was living."

The Old Ones intuitively understood what had happened to the earth in the last twenty thousand years and they knew what had caused John's sickness. It had been a disease of civilization.

Moving the cover aside, John revealed his lower abdomen. A coating of thick mud, the same red color as in the paintings, protected the wound. What Marlise had observed was not a lion eating John, but Lyon destroying John's cancer.

"Look, Marlise. On the wall."

Behind her there was a drawing of the four lions circling John, his guts, colored in red ochre, being torn out and eaten.

"Who painted that?" she wondered.

"You must have," John replied.

There was black pigment all over her hands, one finger was coated with the greasy red ochre and she had smeared some paint on her face.

"Were you scared?" asked Marlise.

"I was terrified, but I couldn't move. As they were becoming real lions, somehow I understood they weren't going to harm me. At least, I hoped so. But when Lyon took a bite out of my stomach I thought that I had been wrong and passed out from the shear terror of the moment, so I didn't feel a thing from then on. I woke up just a little while before you did," John smiled.

***

CHAPTER 7
Fight for Their Lives

L ug, John and Marlise emerged from the cave into a crisp, cool day. The reflection of the sunlight off the snow was strong and the wind blew wisps of snow about them as they wove through the birch on a path they couldn't see but Lug knew well. He stopped them at a small frozen stream and checked the forest for danger before kneeling down to drink, breaking the thin ice with his hand then smiling upward to the icicles still hanging from the trees. They were melting and dripped down on them in these first moments of spring. Their frozen world was warming again.

Lug held the special bone high into the air, directing its smooth flatness toward the warm energy he felt from the yellow sun. He closed his eyes and yelled "New" with all his might. Lug was performing a rite of passage for the new year and consecrated the event with another deep cut into the bone, making it exactly parallel to the sequence of marks already there. "New," he exclaimed several more times.

It wasn't until that evening when Marlise and John understood the full significance of Lug's act. From the clan's whispering, it seemed that something was about to take place and the cave became alive with the rattling of Lyon's ceremonial bones and a harmonious beating of the bear skull drums. Lug brought Nu from the women's side of the cave and sat her down by the fire where Lyon met them with the sacred hide containing the two Venus figurines. Nu grinned broadly as she removed the covering from her belly revealing a highly advanced pregnancy and the crowd gathered closely around to better see the disclosure. Lug's face beamed his happiness to everyone as he carefully placed the two carved stones on Nu's bare belly, eliciting more exclamations of approval.

"Nu!" Lug yelled to the painted ceiling, his arms outstretched towards the ochre-colored animals watching from above.

"Nu," said everyone in unison.

It was another springtime of mothers having their babies that Lug had recorded outside in the bright new sunlight. By logging the annual event with a quick stroke of his flint knife and shouting out his mate's name to the sacred birch, he had captured the undying power of the sun into their perpetual calendar and thus renewed his clan's life for the next year. His acts were conscious, deliberate and would remain forever sacred.

It was as if Marlise's stone carving that John had given Lug inexorably linked them all together in what Joan had called the great cyclical nature of life. It certainly was a most perfect display of life's continuity, a connection that could never be improved upon, even in the next twenty thousand years.

As Marlise stared at the fire, John stole a long secret look at her, wondering if in another time they, too, might have loved one another. She was attractive, full of life, desirous of new experiences and most of all, unlike his often-disagreeable wife, Marlise liked him for who he was. Unfortunately, there wasn't enough time left.

***

Marlise watched as Lyon used a small wooden tube to blow a red powder on John's face. Then he rattled over the initiate as Lug and the others of the lion clan each took a turn to touch John's anointed head. Marlise's role was now as a witness, not participant, in what would happen here so even as the drumming pulled her into the ceremony she couldn't help but feel more and more separated from John.

As beams of light streaked their transformative power across the cave, the men danced to exhaustion before falling to the floor. She drew John and the other dancers as lion-men thrusting their stone-tipped spears at Nu and the other women who themselves had become transformed into reindeer. She heard the deer snorting and could smell them. The hunters attacked and the deer screamed, thrashing around as they were vanquished by the lion-men who thrust terrible weapons into their bodies, causing everything to be drenched red. She watched in horror until the last reindeer had been killed and the lions had settled down to eat. And in her trembling fright, somehow, Marlise had managed to capture it all in her painting on the wall of their cave.

***

Over the next days, the men of the lion clan taught John hunting fundamentals he would need in pursuit of reindeer. He practiced sharpening flint with spent core fragments, as the untouched variety was much too valuable for a beginner to waste. This skill he was not very good at and his admiration for these men and his great grandmother at Holmes village grew with each failed try or new cut he inflicted upon himself.

The men of the lion clan could best use John as a herder but in the event he had an opportunity to take a reindeer, they had armed him with a wooden spear, its fire-hardened tip sufficiently sharp to kill. As it turned out, he was pretty good at throwing spears and he found that he could heave the weapon in a straight line for about ten meters, so if he were lucky to get that close, its sharpness would likely penetrate a deer's thick winter hide. But using their atlatls, his comrades made his efforts look puny, as they had no problem achieving three times his distance. They didn't have the luxury of a supermarket just around the corner he mused to Marlise.

"Are you feeling better?" Dag wanted to know, as they would not take John on the hunt if he could not keep up.

"I'm fine," John replied. "I'm very happy that Lyon could cure me. I was afraid I was going to die soon."

"Die?"

"Yes, the doctors told me that my disease would kill me." Dag and Lug looked to the shaman Lyon for an explanation, but he shrugged too.

"What does die mean?" Dag asked.

They killed animals and ate them, so they must be familiar with death. However, that's not what Dag was asking. John had witnessed Lyon transform into a lion and then cure his cancer. They had achieved special powers that modern people could not even imagine. Dag was asking John if he believed in the supernatural. Did John believe in God? Did he believe in an afterlife?

"What I mean by die is, when your body stops working."

The men were still puzzled by this explanation so John tried again. "Like when you kill a reindeer and eat him. He is dead."

"Then the reindeer becomes part of me. I become the reindeer. He makes me run fast and strong." Dag thumped on his chest with his two fists and grinned broadly.

"We are of the same spirit as the reindeer," said Lyon. "That's why we can find them hiding by the trees and when we call them they join us. And, when our bodies no longer walk on the earth, we are with them," Lyon said, pointing to the reindeer painted on the ceiling.

"In the paintings?" John asked.

"Yes. The reindeer live among us even now, as we sit here by the fire, just as the lion walks among us. The paintings appear on the wall after we chase them, when we remember them, and we will be on the wall, with them," Lyon explained.

These people moved freely between their world and the world of the animals and, despite Lug's annual ritual updating the bone calendar, there was no time for them. No past or future, only the present, and it would remain forever so. Joan had told him to forget about time in a straight line and think of it as a circle. How else could they be here now with the lion people? How could he have been transformed by the magical dance into a lion-man that hunted reindeer? None of this was a ritual. This was an authentic experience. It was not imaginary. It was real.

***

Nu had given him clothing made from reindeer hide and decorated his head with bits of fur and antler. Marlise said he looked like an Indian, which made him feel kind of special, but with the sun shining bright,

John had worked up quite a sweat inside that suit of heavy leather as he tried to keep up with the hunters pushing ever forward in the deep snow. Making matters more uncomfortable, the frozen reindeer droppings he had rubbed onto his body to disguise his scent had melted and now smelled bad. He hoped that the stink would wash off before he was on that long transatlantic airplane flight back to Boston.

Dag had instructed him to keep a hundred meters back from the other hunters, as they could not afford accidentally spooking the herd. Thinking back to when they started out, John believed he would be able to keep up with them, but these men were very fit and he soon let go of that ambition. He didn't want to lose sight of them though, as he had no idea of where he was and knew he couldn't find his way back alone. But they wouldn't leave him out here and the more he thought about it during his rest breaks in the snow, the more sure he was that they had intended for him to lag behind so he wouldn't screw up the hunt.

Ahead, in the distance, he could now see the herd of dark colored reindeer against the white snow. Some lion-men started running into the herd, some heading into the woods, with others fanning out into the adjacent meadow to flank the reindeer's escape. Dag was closest to the herd and was the first to throw his spear. The deer flopped over dead and Dag was upon it almost as it hit the snow, yanking his spear out of the creature and immediately throwing it into another's flank, wasting no energy at all.

John remained fifty meters back from the action, watching the killing and then the butchering that began as soon as the animals fell. He was glad he had not screwed up today's hunt. That it would be a long hard walk back dragging the carcasses along in the snow was acknowledged by everyone so they worked quickly, all wanting to commence the arduous journey as soon as possible and not end up walking too long into the cold night.

He watched as a massive dark hulk crashed out from the trees and he saw its huge teeth gleaming in the bright sunlight. The creature's enormous growl shook John even as far away as he was.

"Lug!" John screamed. "A bear!"

But Lug already knew of the serious trouble and, turning to face the attacking monster that had its own plan for the reindeer, put his spear at the ready as the bear that stood twice as high as he did approached him on its hind legs. John was the closest to Lug, but he didn't know what to do and fear had frozen him in his tracks. Finally, he managed to take a few small steps toward the great battle now taking place.

Lug stabbed the bear over and over, making it roar louder with each deep incursion of the spear's thick wooden shaft. John slowly made his way closer to the action, staying in the trees and hoping the bear wouldn't see him approach. He had no idea how to help Lug and stood paralyzed with fear but a few meters away and, not knowing what else to do but watch the great fight before him, he saw the bear backhand Lug, knocking him hard to the ground. There he lay, stunned, as the bear readied his aim intending to tear Lug to pieces. John rushed forward and, with all his might, shoved his spear deep into the bear, yielding a most deafening response from the huge beast. John had hoped this would stop the bear from killing Lug and give him a chance to get out of its grasp.

The bear, spying John within its reach, swept the full force of an immense paw against him, ripping through his face and killing him instantly. It was the bear's last act, however, as the other hunters were immediately upon it, plunging their weapons into the bear until it, too, was dead.

Now, the bear's blood melted into a small red pond, and the mass of reindeer carcasses strewn about, Lug's torn arm bleeding profusely and John, only partly recognizable, lying dead next to the bear, made a ghastly scene in the once white snow.

***

It was a long, sad journey to the cave from where they had all started out earlier that sunny spring day. Lyon rattled over John's body all the way back, even continuing the rite as they crawled through the passageways, and increasing the fury of the clattering after they put John down by the fire. Nu rushed over, not yet sure how serious it was, but her examination made it completely obvious that all she could do now was to wash his mangled face and try to make him look a little more like John. In her grief, Marlise shook uncontrollably, hiding from the horror in her place at the back of their cave.

The final ceremony began as Lug and Dag solemnly beat their drums and Lyon rattled and chanted over the dead man. Though still shocked by John's appearance, Marlise finally found the courage to sit beside him and she tried her best to look beyond the great claw marks that greatly disfigured his once pleasant features. She cried, holding John's hand as Nu held her close, rocking them back and forth as she would with her coming baby.

At last, the drumming stopped and everyone moved away from the body, leaving John alone in Lyon's sacred care. He shook his bone rattles forcefully, moving round and round about John's corpse, and then pausing above John's head, Lyon prayed upward to the painted ceiling.

"He runs with the lions and chases the reindeer. The bear is now his friend and will not harm him." He rattled again over John.

"John!" Lug proclaimed to the gods, shaking his spear to the heavens.

***

"The bear was hunting the reindeer, too," Lug explained to Marlise. "He surprised me. I should have known better." Lug looked away from her eyes, but the massive claw marks on his arm told not of cowardice but of the expected hazards of living in the natural world. "As the bear was going to kill me, John thrust his spear into its side. The bear killed him instead of me."

She could see it all now. Lug had been thrown to the ground and would be dead if John had not acted. The kinship he felt for these men drove him to his desperate act and there was precious little time to consider what could happen to him.

Lug put his arms around Marlise, engulfing her inside his blood-soaked clothing and the rest of the clan joined in, one-by-one, piling onto the living human core. She could hardly breathe and felt the strangest of sensations, her body tingling with a weird energy. At first, she thought she was suffocating under the weight of the clan, but then it was as if she were disappearing into them, merging into their bodies. She felt the warm comfort of all of their souls surging into her, protecting and calming the uncontrollable trembling that had overtaken her.

Slowly, Marlise fell asleep, not caring if she was in fact dying, as it didn't seem to matter anyway. If she did wake up, perhaps she would be here with this clan of stone-age people, still in the shamanic trance that had brought her and John to them. Alternatively, maybe she would remember all that had happened to her and John as a dream, although a dream so real she would have to check her notes and tape recordings and would carefully ask others what they knew about where she and John had been for these past days. In this latter case, John would be with her and they could discuss what they had both experienced.

***

CHAPTER 8
Remembering John

Joan, is it too late to talk?"

"It's late, Dick. What's wrong?"

"Have you heard from John?"

"John Holmes?"

"Yes."

"No. Why?"

"I haven't heard a word since he went to France. That's months ago?"

"Do you think he, uh?" Joan asked.

"Died?" Dick replied.

"Yes," answered Joan.

"No. I don't think so. Not yet, anyway. It would be another six months."

"I'm sure his sessions with Marlise went fine. Come to think of it, though, I haven't heard from her either, but that doesn't mean anything. She may not get to her report for a while. Maybe he's with his friend Henri, carousing around Paris," she said trying to comfort him.

"Maybe," Dick replied solemnly.

"Oh, come on Dick, that would be good for the man."

"Let's hope that's what he's doing," Dick replied, a little perkier than before. "I'd like to see him have some fun, before he."

"Stop worrying so much. You're a good doctor. John's fine, you'll see. Look, I have to travel tomorrow but you call me at the end of the week. If you haven't heard from John by then, I'll call Marlise and we'll track him down, okay?"

"All right, Joan. Sorry."

"Go to sleep."

"I think I'll try the proverbial glass of warm milk."

"Good night, Dick."

***

The warm milk didn't work as well as Dick had hoped it would and he spent the whole night tossing and turning as he worried about what happened to John. He imagined every possible scenario from a mugging in the dark alleys of Paris to a car accident on some out-of the-way road in the French countryside. Perhaps, he was struggling with the medical eventualities brought on by his cancer and was confined to his deathbed in a French hospital, unable to effectively communicate with the doctors and nurses. It was almost dawn when, as a sliver of orange light crept into his Cambridge apartment and released the winter night, he finally fell asleep and the nightmare began.

***

"I'm going to die," John announced from the couch across the room.

Dick could see John was upset and that made it all the more difficult to stop laughing.

"I want to discover the true meaning of life," John added.

Dick's laughter only got louder when John asked him to stop.

"I mean my life, not everybody's life," John shouted in desperation.

Dick had to look away in order to get control of himself. When he had finally calmed down and wiped the tears of laughter from his eyes, instead of seeing John across the room, he found himself standing in the middle of an immense, old cemetery. There were tombstones of every description, large and small, very old and some new, all crowding into the place for as far as one could see. The dim yellow streetlights provided just enough light so he could read the name at the new grave in front of him.

"John Holmes. 1949-2007," he read aloud. Then he heard the laughing. It grew louder and louder. "Who would be laughing in a cemetery?"

he wondered, listening carefully to the voice. It was his own laughter, uncontrollably mocking John. Dick closed his eyes and pushed his hands tight against the sides of his head, desperately trying to block out his own cruel and annoying laugh. Why didn't he help John discover the meaning of his life? Would he be forever tortured by his failure to help this poor departed soul? It was one of his few mistakes in forty years of practice but maybe it wasn't that big of a deal, after all. It wasn't really possible to discover the ultimate meaning of one's life and it had been a ridiculous question for John to ask. Dick clenched his eyes and squeezed his hands over his ears.

Eventually, the laughter faded away and he peaked out, afraid the laughing would begin again. He decided he must still be in the cemetery, noticing the yellowish glow. But it wasn't until he opened his eyes all the way that he realized he was in a cave. Slowly, his eyes adjusted to the dim light and Dick saw the ancient paintings of bison, deer with large antlers, horses and a ferocious but somewhat weird looking group of lions. It was a magnificent place, subdued yet colorful and eerily captivating.

Suddenly, that hair-raising chill that tells you that someone is creeping up from behind came over him. He could feel its presence but was too scared to move. If he turned around, he would have to face it, and he expected he would see some terrible creature, holding a crude, terrible weapon, ready to impale him in the guts. Overwhelming fear kept him frozen in place until he heard it. The sound came from behind. "Crack." There it was again. It was a fire and John was lying by it and alive Dick realized with great relief. He was about to call out to him just as half a dozen men dressed in animal skins crawled into the cave. As quietly as he could, Dick backed into the shadows and held his breath, hoping they wouldn't see him. Slowly, he slid down to the cool stone floor and watched. He couldn't hear what they were saying but he was relieved that it seemed they weren't going to come after him, at least not yet.

The cavemen began to dance around the fire and bang on drums. In their lion skull headdresses they looked very much like the strange lions that were painted on the ceiling. Dick watched, captivated, completely forgetting he was an intruder and that these lion-men could easily kill and eat him if they wanted to. One of the dancers pounced on John's body and began tearing at his flesh, blood dripping from the lion-man's mouth as he pulled at his belly. Dick closed his eyes, knowing he would be next.

To his pleasant surprise, when he opened his eyes after a long time of keeping them tightly closed, Dick found himself standing in the middle of a field of snow with a cold wind blowing in his face. Several hundred meters away, he saw a man running towards others who were similarly dressed in animal skins. Dick shrunk down so he could watch them without being seen and became so totally occupied with the surreal vision of these silent distant figures in the bright landscape that at first he didn't notice the large dark figure emerge from the woods. It knocked one of the men to the ground and, as Dick looked on, another hunter ran up and thrust a spear deep into the animal's side. Dick couldn't hear the crunch of bones or howls and screams of pain from where the action was taking place because he was too far away. He could see bursts of red blood spit out on the snow as the brutal drama continued across that white frozen space.

The panting grew louder as the giant bear now came to get him. He fled in the deep snow as fast as he could but the animal quickly gained ground on him as he desperately tried to reach the trees before the bear got him. With each crunching footstep in the snow his acute dread of the ultimate outcome so dramatically increased that it was all Dick could do to keep from screaming out loud. The bear caught him by his leg and pulled him down off the tree before he could climb high enough to get away. Its drooling mouth full of gleaming white fangs roared at him and Dick realized he would be dead in a second.

"Beep. Beep. Beep. Beep. Beep. Beep. Beep. Beep."

His eyes burst open to the bleak gray sky that showed through the crack between the curtains. In soaking wet sheets, still under the spell of the horrifying nightmare, Dick gasped for breath as he struggled to roll over and turn the alarm off. It was eight-thirty in the morning in Cambridge, and for that reality he would be eternally grateful. It must have been only a bad dream.

***

"Patient visit summary for John Holmes, dated November 30," Dick said into the microphone. "We discussed his plans going forward and I'm reminded by those boats and the cold wind across the water that it was almost a year ago when John and I first met."

There was a knock at the door and Joan Hanover peaked in with her usual friendly smile. Dick clicked off the tape recorder and motioned for her to come in.

"Joan, this letter came today. I haven't opened it yet," he said with a look of dread on his face. "It's from Dr. Pomard."

"Why didn't you read it?"

"I thought I would wait for you. He was your patient, too." Dick could tell she doubted that was the true reason behind his hesitation. "To be totally honest," he admitted, "I think it contains bad news and I didn't want to read it alone."

"Dick, you're always thinking the worst. Just because we haven't heard from John, or Marlise for that matter, it doesn't mean that something bad has happened to him."

"It's been too long."

"Okay. Let's read what Marlise has to say."

The letter was addressed to Richard Amico, M.D., and began with the typical professional details of the case, including references to the dates Dr. Pomard had met with John in France. It was the letter they had been waiting for.

"This is my report on your patient Mr. John Holmes. I am very sorry that it has taken me so long to send this letter to you." Dick sighed and Joan gave him a look that told him to relax, again. "I would very much appreciate it if you would share this communication with my friend and colleague Dr. Joan Hanover," read Dick. "John was a perfect patient and I was very pleased to have known him. In fact, I had the most remarkable experience because of my participation in his therapy."

"Now, we're getting somewhere. Keep reading," Joan prodded him.

"From the very beginning, when we met at my family's boulangerie in Perigeux, we found ourselves in a relationship of mutual trust and friendship, which I partly attribute to his love for our French culture. He shared with me the intimacies of his times in Paris with his friend Henri Honoré, whom by the way, I have met once and who happens to be a very famous artist. John told me about carousing around Paris with Henri, which I must say was surely very innocent. Both men are complete gentlemen, even though I am sure they often drank more than they should have."

"You see Dick, I told you that John was having fun with his old friend in Paris," Joan remarked.

"Yes, you did," he replied, glancing out at the gray Boston sky. "One evening, apparently when they were making their way from one place to another, they came upon the famous Montparnasse cemetery."

"What?" Dick asked in a surprised voice.

"What's wrong?" asked Joan.

He sat back in his chair and set the letter down on the desk. "The other night, before this letter came, you remember, I called you because I couldn't sleep."

"You were worried about John."

"Well, I didn't go to sleep until almost dawn and then when I did, I had a dream, no a nightmare, that went on for an eternity and scared the hell out of me. It began in a cemetery and I woke up in a cold sweat about to be eaten by a huge bear."

"My goodness," she said, taunting him with a little smirk.

"I was running in a field of deep snow, desperately trying to get away from the creature. I was just about to get away when the bear caught me."

"What happened?"

"Thank God I was saved by the bell."

"What bell?"

"My alarm went off." She laughed and Dick tried to laugh too, but he couldn't. "That's not all," he continued.

"Dick, this sounds to me like a very meaningful dream. We can talk about it later if you like, but don't you think we should finish the letter about John first?"

Ignoring her, he continued on. "I was so shaken by the dream, I wrote it down in my professional journal, before I forgot anything. I think you should read it now."

"Now? Why, was your dream was about John?"

"Yes."

"It was our conversation about him, earlier that evening, that probably set you up for it."

"Maybe, but I think what I dreamt already happened to him, in real life."

"What are you talking about?"

"That's why I want us to stop reading Marlise's letter for a minute so you can read my notes."

"All right, Dick," she agreed, but remaining confused by his mumbling about the dream.

"It will help me keep my sanity." Joan gave him another puzzled look as he grabbed his journal from the top drawer of the desk and handed it to her. "It begins on page 101."

As she began to read, Joan still wasn't sure what had spooked Dick, but they had known one another for a long time and she knew Dick to be a sound, logical professional. If his dream was bothering him this much, it was not because of a bizarre obsession with his patient's welfare but rather because there must be something truly significant behind it.

***

"I agree it was a weird dream," she said closing his journal. "But then, that's what dreams sometimes are, strangely assembled semi-realities."

"Maybe. Now, let's find out what happened to John." He picked up Marlise's letter and continued from where they had left off. "Standing in front of Jean-Paul Sartre's grave in the Montparnasse cemetery they had a conversation about the meaning of life."

"See, you dreamt about John's tombstone, but it was Sartre's they visited," Joan remarked.

The more they read though, the more Dick was convinced that, very strangely indeed, his dream almost perfectly remembered what had happened to John, but Joan still had her doubts. Rather, she believed, though his dream and John's journey was a remarkable coincidence, they were both just dreams.

Dick read on. "I took the enclosed photograph a few weeks ago when for the first time since our journey back to the Old Ones I visited the cave on my family's property in Perigeux. As many times as I had been in that cave, I had never seen this painting before and I have no explanation as to how it came to be on the cave wall, other than I must have drawn it while John and I were with the Old Ones, as remarkable as that sounds. What I am not sure of is when I did this."

"What does she mean by that? Joan asked.

"She must mean that she drew it during her recent visit there with John," Dick suggested.

"It certainly couldn't be that she drew it twenty thousand years ago," Joan shrugged. "Where is John now?" she asked.

"Let me keep reading," Dick asked, clearing his throat. "Before John went on the reindeer hunt, they danced in a ritual around the fire, all of them becoming lions and hunting reindeer right before my eyes. They threw their spears at reindeer women who danced with antlers they held to their heads. It seemed as though the cave men, including John, transformed into real lions and attacked the reindeer with their huge fangs and claws. That's some of what I painted on the wall."

"This photo is absolutely unbelievable. It's like the cave in my dream."

"You know what I was just thinking? How did Marlise have the courage to watch what was happening, especially if she thought it was really occurring?"

"Now you know why I woke up in a cold sweat."

"I don't have first hand experience of exactly what happened to John and these details are based upon what the hunters told me," Marlise said in her letter. "It was spring, but you will remember that during the last Ice Age, the weather was not very warm, so they had to walk through waist-deep snow. They knew that John was inexperienced, but they also needed as much help as possible, so they gave him a spear and told him to stay back. What happened next was told to me by Lug. He had just killed a reindeer when a huge bear ran out from the woods and attacked him. He speared it, but the bear managed to knock him to the ground and was going to kill him when John rushed to his aid and drove his spear into the bear. He was too close and the bear killed him with one swipe of its paw. The hunters killed the bear, and brought back its skull, along with John's body. Lyon told me he rattled over John's body for a long time, but I think this was done out of respect and was not an attempt to revive him. The damage the bear had done was not repairable. Now, please look very closely at the photograph. As you will see, there is the likeness of John, including a scar on his abdomen which I attribute to the cancer surgery done by Lyon."

"It's John spearing the bear," Joan choked. All Dick could do for the moment was to stare at the photograph with tears welling in his eyes.

"I believe that Lug added this last act of John to the painting I made and I think he did so in remembrance of the man who had saved his life. By the way, he would have done so about twenty thousand years ago. I also want you to know that I fulfilled John's promises to the Holmes village, the talking stones in the cave and the sacred tree roots. As I was coming back to this time, I paused and told them all the story of our visit to the Old Ones, including that John had been cured of his cancer. They were all especially proud of John when they learned he had saved Lug's life. We'll talk of John Holmes again, but for now I close my letter about his very remarkable journey. Sincerely, Marlise Pomard."

"I want to see this painting someday," Dick said, staring at the photograph.

"I think you may already have," Joan smiled through her tears.

"John's remarkable journey," Dick smiled. "I'm happy he was able to discover the true meaning of his life. It gives one reason for hope, doesn't it?"

THE END.

***

Made in the USA